The Stonecutter

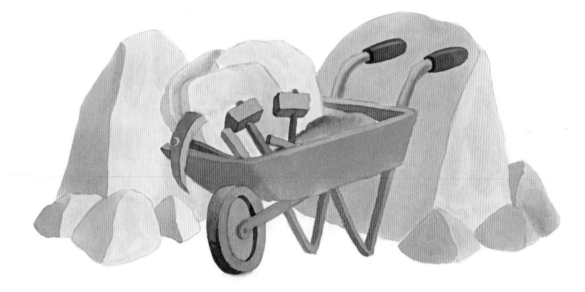

illustrated by Laura Barella

Child's Play (International) Ltd
Ashworth Rd, Bridgemead, Swindon, SN5 7YD UK
Swindon   Auburn ME   Sydney
© 2012 Child's Play (International) Ltd   Printed in Heshan, China
ISBN 978-1-84643-478-5   L140312FUFT06124785
1 3 5 7 9 10 8 6 4 2
www.childs-play.com

Once upon a time there was a stonecutter.
Every day, he went to the mountains to cut stone.

He sold the stone to the people in the town, so that
they could build walls, or houses, or barns, or bridges.
He was a very happy man. He enjoyed his work,
and he loved working in the mountains.

One day, the stonecutter delivered some stone
to a rich family's house. He saw many precious things
there, like silk carpets, comfortable beds, plump
cushions and feather pillows. As he walked home,
he thought of how hard he had worked that day,
and how tired he felt.

"If only I were rich," he thought, "I could have a really comfortable bed! I'd be so happy!"
"Your wish is granted!" said a voice from nowhere.
"Now you, too, are rich!"
The stonecutter looked around, but there was no one to be seen.
"I must be tired," he thought.
"I'm dreaming in my sleep!"

When the stonecutter arrived home, he thought he was still dreaming. Instead of his humble cottage, there was a large palace, filled with beautiful things. It was just like the rich family's house.

The stonecutter was happy being rich for a while. He lay all day in his splendid bed, while servants did all the work.

One afternoon, however, he was feeling bored. Looking out of the window, he saw a prince passing by in a golden carriage. One servant was keeping him cool with a fan, while another held an umbrella above his head to protect him from the fierce sun.

"If only I were a prince, I'd be so happy!"
thought the stonecutter. "I would have a carriage,
and servants with fans and umbrellas!"

"Your wish is granted!" said the voice from nowhere.
"Now you, too, are such a prince!"
Suddenly, the stonecutter heard the sound of
wheels. He was delighted to see a golden coach
outside his house. It was pulled by four large horses,
and surrounded by servants.

He jumped aboard at once, and bade them take him for a ride. He lay back in the coach. Some servants kept him cool with fans, and others held umbrellas above his head.

Sometimes, the stonecutter drove around the town in his splendid coach. He would see the people working hard in the market. On other days, he would drive out to the countryside, to watch the farmers working hard in their fields. "How happy I am!" he thought. "I could live like this for ever!"

After a while, however, he began to feel bored and unhappy again.

"My servants water my lawns every day," he thought, "but the sun still scorches them. And even though my servants hold umbrellas above my head, my face still burns. It's not fair! The sun is much more powerful than me."

"If only I were the sun, I'd be so happy!"
"Your wish is granted!" said the voice from nowhere.
"Now you are the sun!"
No sooner did he look around to see where the voice
had come from, than the stonecutter found himself
high in the sky, throwing out beams of light.

He was very happy with his new powers.
He brought the dawn to sleepers, and his light helped
trees and flowers and crops to grow. After a while,
though, he became bored and unhappy once again.
And one day, when a cloud hid him from the earth,
he lost his temper altogether.

"It's not fair!" he thought. "This cloud is more important than me! If only I were a cloud, I'd be so happy!"

"Your wish is granted!" said the voice from nowhere. "Now you are a cloud!"

The stonecutter loved being a cloud. He hid the sun's rays from the earth when he felt like it, and when he rained he loved to see the flowers and the crops grow. Sometimes, he rained and rained so much that the rivers overflowed, and bridges, buildings, walls and fields were all swept away. Only the mountain rocks did not move.

"It's not fair!" he thought. "The rock is more important than I am. If only I were the rock, I'd be so happy!" "Your wish is granted," said the voice from nowhere. "Now you are the rock!"

He enjoyed being the rock. The sun could not burn him, and the rain could not wash him away. "Nothing can move me!" he thought. "Now, I am more powerful than anything else!"

One day, however, the stonecutter heard a strange chipping noise. He felt a strange tingling, and looked down to see someone cutting out a large stone from the rock at his feet. Even as he watched, the block of stone fell away.

"It's not fair!" he thought. "They are more important than me. If only I were a stonecutter, I'd be so happy!"

"Your wish is granted," said the voice from nowhere. "Now you are a stonecutter once again!" The stonecutter looked down. He was himself once again, dressed in his old working clothes. He rushed home, to find his large palace had disappeared. In its place was his old cottage. His carriage and all the servants were gone. Only his old tools remained, back in the shed, ready to be used again. "Back to work!" he thought. "It's not so bad after all!"

The stonecutter went back to stonecutting again, and found happiness in his work.
"I was never really happy being rich or powerful," he would think to himself, "because I always wanted to be something else. A stonecutter is what I am, and I'll be happy cutting stone for the rest of my life!"